For Eugenie

"Happy Birthday"
Mikey
Grandma Teddi xo
& Bill xo
Grandpa 1999

SIMON & SCHUSTER
BOOKS FOR YOUNG READERS
Simon & Schuster Building, Rockefeller Center
1230 Avenue of the Americas, New York, New York 10020

SIMON & SCHUSTER BOOKS FOR YOUNG READERS
is a trademark of Simon & Schuster.
The text of this book is set in 16 pt. Stempel Schneidler.
Manufactured in Great Britain.

10 9 8 7 6 5 4 3 2 1

ISBN: 0-671-73474-1

Budgie
Goes to Sea

H.R.H. The Duchess of York
Illustrated by John Richardson

SIMON & SCHUSTER BOOKS FOR YOUNG READERS
PUBLISHED BY SIMON & SCHUSTER
NEW YORK LONDON TORONTO SYDNEY TOKYO SINGAPORE

One day Budgie, the little helicopter, was chatting with his friend Pippa, the Piper Warrior plane. He told her he had been given the exciting new job of postman.

"Nothing exciting about that!" said Pippa. "We all carry mail from time to time."

"But you couldn't do *this* job," crowed Budgie, "because you can't land on a naval ship at sea."

"I could do it easily," said Pippa.

"If you could deliver this mail," protested Budgie, "I'd...I'd have a bath!" Budgie, you see, hated baths. He much preferred being dirty.

"Well," said Pippa, "if the ship is an aircraft carrier, you are going to be very clean indeed."

Budgie worried about that until his radio came on. "Control to Budgie. We have an important shipment of spare parts for the fleet and the wind is beginning to blow. If they don't get these parts, their rescue aircraft won't be able to fly. Please prepare to leave at once."

As Budgie lifted off with his cargo net full, Pippa called to him, "Good luck and I'll see you at the wash when you get back." Fergus, the cat, just sniggered.

"Blatter. Clatter. Blatter." Budgie flew over the coast. The wind
began to blow harder. A line of black clouds hung on the
horizon.

"Control to Budgie. The weather is getting worse. Deliver your parts to the destroyer Camballtown, and return home immediately."

As Budgie approached the destroyer, the wind began to blow even harder. Looking down, Budgie saw that the ship's own helicopter covered half the landing area.

Budgie turned into the wind and began to lower his packages onto the deck. Just as they touched down, a huge gust of wind blew the cargo against the side of the landing platform.

Budgie pulled up with all his might and barely missed crashing into the ship.

"Destroyer to Budgie. That was too close. Land on the aircraft carrier instead."

"Roger," said Budgie, trying to use his strongest voice. He did not want to have a bath, but he did feel a bit shaky from his near miss.

Budgie touched down on the big carrier. The deck was covered with jets. Budgie felt small, but he was proud to be doing his job for the navy.

The crew unfastened his cargo net and Budgie lifted off for the flight home. As he pulled up, the sky darkened and it began to rain.

Suddenly Budgie's radio came on. "Man overboard! Man overboard!" Looking down as he flew back over the destroyer, Budgie could see men lowering a lifeboat. He watched as the wind slammed the little boat against the side of the ship.

"Destroyer to Budgie! Destroyer to Budgie! We cannot launch our lifeboat. We have a man overboard and our helicopter is broken. Can you help?"

Budgie gulped. "I'm not big enough for this," he thought, "and
the wind is too strong and the waves are huge." But Budgie
knew he had to try. He called the destroyer, pretending not to
be afraid. "I'll do what I can."

Budgie began to search the sea behind the destroyer. The waves and the rain made it hard to see anything.

Finally he saw a beam of light. It must be a rescue flashlight,
Budgie thought as he moved closer.

In the sea, the sailor was struggling to stay afloat.

"Keep swimming. I'm going to let down a rope ladder," shouted Budgie as the waves roared below. "Don't give up!"

For a minute Budgie thought he was too late. The sailor had sunk below the surface. Budgie could only see his arm above water.

With the wind howling Budgie dropped as low as he could. He could feel the spray from the waves on his skids. With one final pass he dragged his ladder in front of the sailor.

"Grab hold," Budgie yelled and pushed his engines to full power.

The sailor held on as hard as he could, and Budgie circled back toward the ships.

Budgie lowered the man carefully to the ship's deck as all his mates cheered. Once his ladder was released, Budgie immediately lifted off and flew toward home. The wind was still very strong and Budgie just hoped he could make it back to the field.

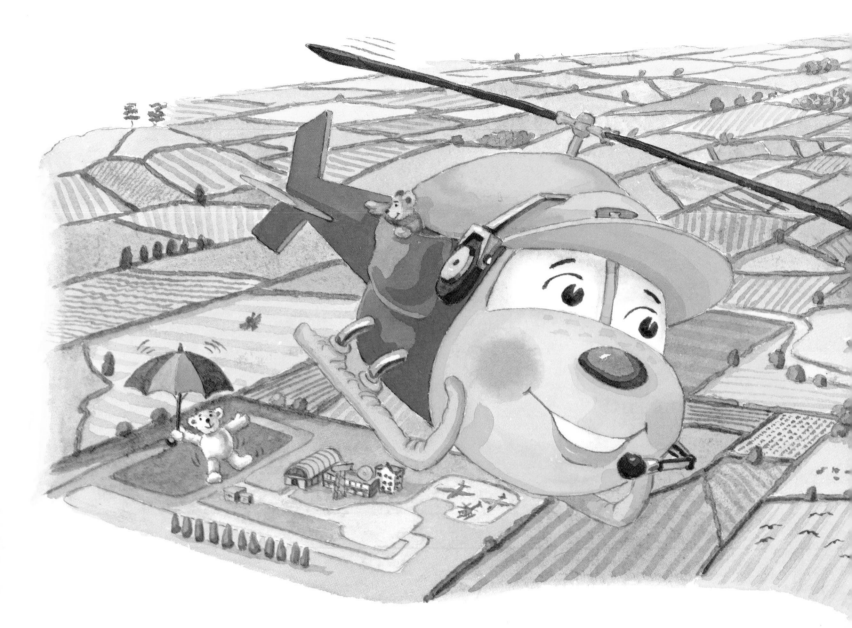

When Budgie finally arrived there, Pippa, Lionel the Lynx helicopter, and Chin-up, the Chinook, were waiting. They had heard everything on the radio.

"We are all *so* proud of you," cried Pippa.

"Hurumph," Lionel said, "that wasn't a bad job Budgie."

"Grrreat stuff," said Chin-up as he chewed his gum.

After everyone had finished praising Budgie, he had a chat
with Pippa.

"Pippa, you won our bet. You could have landed on that aircraft carrier. I guess I'd better have that wash now."

"I could never have saved that man, Budgie," Pippa said, "so I'm calling our bet off."

Now this was a special day indeed thought Budgie. All this adventure and no bath before bed!